D1562027

The Only Friend

by Kim Kane

Illustrated by Jon Davis

PICTURE WINDOW BOOKS

a capstone imprint

To my dear friend Nic and her daughter
(and my goddaughter), Maya.

— Kim

Ginger Green, Playdate Queen is published by Picture Window Books,
A Capstone Imprint
1710 Roe Crest Drive
North Mankato, Minnesota 56003
www.mycapstone.com

Ginger Green, Playdate Queen — *The Only Friend*
Text Copyright © 2016 Kim Kane
Illustration Copyright © 2016 Jon Davis
Series Design Copyright © 2016 Hardie Grant Egmont
First published in Australia by Hardie Grant Egmont 2016

All rights reserved. No part of this publication may be reproduced in
whole or in part, or stored in a retrieval system, or transmitted in any
form or by any means, electronic, mechanical, photocopying, recording,
or otherwise, without written permission of the publisher.

Library of Congress Cataloging-in-Publication data
is available on the Library of Congress website.
978-1-5158-1950-9 (library binding)
978-1-5158-2018-5 (eBook PDF)

Summary: Ginger is playing with Maya today. But what happens when
Maya wants to play with Ginger's sister instead?

Designers: Mack Lopez and Russell Griesmer
Production specialist: Tori Abraham

Printed and bound in China.
010734S18

Table of Contents

Chapter
One

My name is Ginger Green.

I am seven years old.

I am the Playdate Queen!

Today my friend **Maya** is
coming over after school.

Last night I called Maya.

I said, "Maya, this is Ginger Green, Playdate Queen. Would you like to come to my house and play with me?"

Maya said,

"YES!"

After school, Mom picks up my sister Violet, Maya, and me.

She has Penny in the stroller.

Penny is my little sister, and she is naked.

"Why is your sister naked?"
asks Maya.

says Violet.
She looks at
Mom.

11

"Do you have a little brother or sister, Maya?" asks Mom.

"No," says Maya. "I am an only child. I have no sisters and no brothers."

How nice, I think.

Mom puts a blanket over Penny.

"Who would like a cookie?"

asks Mom.

Mom is good at playdates.

She holds out a lunch box.
Inside are four chocolate cookies.

"No, thanks," says Violet. "I don't like chocolate."

"Guests first," Mom says to Maya.

"No, thanks," says Maya. "I don't like chocolate either."

Mom looks at me.
She looks
surprised.

I am surprised. This is not true.

I am Ginger
Green, Playdate
Queen, and I
know Maya likes
chocolate.

I know Maya likes chocolate cookies. I know this because Maya told me chocolate cookies were her **favorite** food.

And I told Mom.

"I don't like them either," I say.

"Oh, well," says Mom. "More for Dad and me."

"And me!" says Penny.

Mom hands Penny a cookie. Penny does not like clothes, but she does like chocolate cookies.

Chapter Two

When we get home, Mom makes Penny take a bath. Violet dumps her bag in the playroom.

Violet always dumps her bag
when she gets home. Then
she always reads.

"Let's play
dress-up,"

I say to Maya.

"Great," says Violet.

I stop. I was not talking to Violet.

"Great," says Maya. She is looking at Violet.

"Violet, go read," I say. "You are too bossy to play dress-up."

"No, I'm not," says Violet.

"No, she's not," says
Maya.

Maya smiles
up at Violet.

I am confused. But I don't
say, "I am confused."

Instead I say, "OK."

I pick up a princess hat.

"What do you want to wear?"

I ask Maya.

Maya picks a pink dress with ruffles, a long wig, and a wand.

Violet takes the hat from me.

"That's mine,"

I say.

Violet puts on the hat.

I try to grab it, but she is too tall.

Violet is **two** years older.

She is **two** years smarter.

She is also **two** years taller.

I pick up a book.

I THROW IT
AT THE PRINCESS HAT.

I miss.

"MOM!" I yell.

"Make Violet go away. We're playing dress-up, and she's being bossy!"

"NO, I'M NOT!" shouts Violet.

"No, she's not!" shouts Maya.

I look at Maya. I am Ginger Green, Playdate Queen. I invited Maya to MY house. I invited her to play with ME.

I did NOT invite Maya to play with Violet.

Violet straightens the princess hat.

"I am the fairy queen,"
she says. "Maya is the
fairy princess. Ginger,
you are the toad."

Violet hands me the toad mask.

"I am not a toad," I say.

I am so ANGRY.

I AM SO ANGRY THAT
I AM
SHAKING.

I jump up and HIT the princess hat off Violet's head.

 **"Ow,"** says Violet.

She snatches the hat back.

I look at Maya. I want Maya to say NO. I want her to say Ginger Green is not a toad. Ginger Green is already a queen.

But Maya does not say anything.
I am so angry, I want to snatch
Maya back like Violet snatched
back the princess hat.

I turn and

run to my room.

I go to my bed, and I cry.

I am Ginger Green, Playdate Queen. It is not Violet Green, Playdate Queen. Violet has books. I have playdates.

I can hear Violet-the-friend-snatcher and Maya-who-did-not-say-no playing.

"Fairy Princess, you may make a wish!"

"Thank you, Fairy Queen!"

But I am Ginger Green, Playdate
Queen, and a playdate queen
always joins in.

Then I look up and
see my green tights.
I see my flippers.

Chapter
Three

I pick up the mask and put it on. Then I hop back to the playroom.

"Terrific," says Violet when
she sees me hopping.
"You'll be the toad."

I wipe my eyes. Maya sees.
She gives me a hug.

I am still angry with Violet.
I am still angry with Maya.
My feelings are hurt.

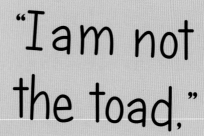

"I am not the toad,"

I say.

I stand proud in my tights, mask, and flippers.

"I am a frog," I say.
I say it coolly and calmly.

"A toad is the color of snot. A toad has warts. But a frog? A frog is a beautiful emerald-green color. A frog doesn't have warts at all."

Maya laughs. Maya laughs
like she means it.

I laugh too.

"Very funny," says
Violet. "You can be
a frog then. Now
let's play fairy tale."

Maya looks at me and laughs even harder. I laugh even harder too. We laugh so much we both cry. But this time I am happy-crying.

"You girls are too silly
for me," says Violet.

She goes back
to her book.

"Violet, stop! Let's play with the dollhouse then,"

I say.

I do not like it when Violet is a friend-snatcher, but I do not want her to feel left out. I know what it's like to be left out.

"No, thanks," says Violet.

"I am going to read."

I ask.

says Violet.

Maya and I go back into the
bedroom and sit down at the
dollhouse.

"Cute dollhouse," says Maya.

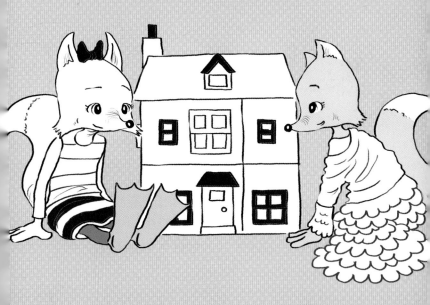

"Thanks," I say. "I built it with Violet. We even sewed the curtains."

"Wow," says Maya.

On the tiny bed is a tiny baby doll. I made it from a cork and a piece of felt.

"Do you want to be the mom?" asks Maya. "Or the baby?"

"The mom," I say.

Penny comes into the bedroom with a towel on her head.

"OK," says Maya. "I'll be the baby. But the baby cannot be alone. The baby needs two sisters."

"The baby can have two sisters,"
I say. "One sister is bossy. And
one sister is naked."

Maya smiles. "Bossy is better
than lonely. Onlies are
sometimes lonely."

"At least onlies don't have naked sisters," I say, pointing at Penny.

Maya laughs. "No, but onlies don't have anyone to build dollhouses with either."

I look at the baby doll.

It does look lonely.

"I share my dress-up clothes with you, Maya," I say. "I share my dollhouse with you. I can share my sisters with you too. Some days, you can even have them."

Maya grins.

I grin too. Maya is my friend after all.

Maya does not like
Violet better
than me.

Maya just likes Violet
because she doesn't have
any sisters of her own.

I am Ginger Green, Playdate Queen, and I share with my friends.

I will even share
my sisters.

THE END

Glossary

bossy—fond of ordering people around

confused—feeling unclear or uncertain about something

fairy tale—a simple children's story about imaginary beings

invite—to ask someone to do something or go somewhere

lonely—feeling alone or having no company

stroller—a chair on wheels in which a baby or young child can be pushed along

wand—a slender rod used in performing magic

About the Author and Illustrator

Kim Kane is an award-winning author who writes for children and teens in Australia and overseas. Kim's books include the CBCA short-listed picture book *Family Forest* and her middle-grade novel *Pip: the Story of Olive*. Kim lives with her family in Melbourne, Australia, and writes whenever and wherever she can.

Kim Kane

Pirates, old elephants, witches in bloomers, bears on bikes, ugly cats, sweet kids — Jon Davis does it all! Based in Twickenham, United Kingdom, Jon Davis has illustrated more than forty kids' books for publishers across the globe.

Jon Davis

Collect them all!